AMERICAN LEGENDS™

Sojourner Truth

Frances E. Ruffin

For my father, who has always inspired me with his enthusiasm for learning.

Published in 2002 by The Rosen Publishing Group, Inc.
29 East 21st Street, New York, NY 10010

Distributed to the School Market by
Newbridge Educational Publishing
33 Boston Post Road West, Suite 440
Marlborough, MA 01752
1-800-867-0307

Copyright © 2002 by The Rosen Publishing Group, Inc.

All rights reserved. No part of this book may be reproduced in any form without permission in writing from the publisher, except by a reviewer.

First Edition

Book Design: Michael de Guzman

Project Editor: Kathy Campbell

Photo Credits: pp. 4, 15 © Bettmann/CORBIS; p. 7 © Jules T. Allen/CORBIS; p. 8 © The Corcoran Gallery of Art/CORBIS; p. 11 © The Granger Colection, New York; pp. 12, 16, 19 © North Wind Pictures; p. 20 © National Portrait Gallery, Smithsonian Institution/Art Resource.

Ruffin, Frances E.
 Sojourner Truth / Frances Ruffin.
     p. cm. — (American legends)
 Includes bibliographical references and index.
 ISBN 0-8239-5826-4 (lib. bdg.)   ISBN 978-1-4007-1754-5 (paperback)
 1. Truth, Sojourner, d. 1883—Juvenile literature. 2. African American abolitionists—Biography—Juvenile literature.
 3. African American women—Biography—Juvenile literature. 4. Abolitionists—United States—Biography—Juvenile literature.
 5. Social reformers—United States—Biography—Juvenile literature. [1. Truth, Sojourner, d. 1883. 2. Abolitionists.
 3. Reformers. 4. African Americans—Biography. 5. Women—Biography.] I. Title. II. American legends (New York, N.Y.)
 E185.97.T8 R84 2002
 305.5'67'092—dc21   2001000143

Printed by Corporate Graphics, Inc.
Manufactured in North Mankato, Minnesota USA
January 2016
Rosen PO#: 010616CGn
Sundance/Newbridge PO#: 510914

Seth Hawkins, his shop, and the other characters in this book are fictional, but the details in this story about Colonial wigmakers and Colonial life are true.

Contents

1	Sojourner Truth	5
2	What Is a Legend?	6
3	A Slave Named Isabella	9
4	Sold Away	10
5	A Young Marriage	13
6	Saving Peter from Slavery	14
7	Freedom!	17
8	A New Name	18
9	Speaking Out	21
10	On the Road with a Message	22
	Glossary	23
	Index	24
	Web Sites	24

This picture of Sojourner Truth was printed often on postcards. She sold the postcards to raise money for the speeches she gave around the country. Although she was born into slavery in 1797, Sojourner became a free woman at age 30 in 1827.

Sojourner Truth

Sojourner Truth was born a child of slaves in 1797. Slaves were people who were "owned" by other people and were forced to work without pay. At a very young age, Sojourner was forced to become a slave. She was sold and bought many times and made to work hard in the fields and the homes of her owners. She fought until 1827 to become a free woman. The word "sojourn" means living in a place for a while, then traveling on. During her long lifetime, Sojourner Truth lived in many places, then traveled on. During her travels, Sojourner Truth became a famous spokesperson for women's rights and **civil rights**. A former slave, she became a **legend** while fighting for the freedom of others.

What Is a Legend?

A legend can be a story from the past. Legends are handed down through the years. A legend also can be a person who becomes the center of stories. These legends are often heroes. Sojourner Truth is an example of a hero. She was known for her bravery and her wisdom. After working hard with her hands for many years, she spent the rest of her life working as an **abolitionist** and a **feminist**. Although Sojourner could neither read nor write, she could quote almost every word from the Bible. She became famous for her stirring speeches about equal rights for all Americans.

It is fun to read legends, or stories that come down to us from the past. Some legends are about famous people, such as Sojourner Truth. The stories about Sojourner center on the qualities that she had as a great speaker and leader against slavery.

This painting shows an area north of New York City and along the Hudson River. Sojourner Truth was born on a farm in Hurley, New York, near the Hudson River.

A Slave Named Isabella

Sojourner Truth was born in 1797, on a farm near the Hudson River, north of New York City. Her parents named her Isabella, but 46 years later she changed her name to Sojourner Truth. That is the name by which she is known today. Sojourner was the second youngest of Elizabeth and James Baumfree's 10 children. Her parents were slaves who had been born in Africa and had been brought to America to work. Sojourner knew only her brother Peter. Her sisters and other brothers were taken from her parents while they were young to work for other **masters**. Sojourner's mother told her that no matter how difficult her life became, "There is a God in the sky who hears and sees you."

Sold Away

For many years, Sojourner spoke only Dutch. The man who had owned Sojourner's family was from Holland and spoke Dutch. Sojourner was removed from her family when the owner died in 1808. She was **auctioned** off and sold to new masters, the Nealys, who paid $100 for her and a flock of sheep. Sojourner was only 11 years old, but she was very tall for her age. The Nealys were cruel to Sojourner. They spoke English instead of Dutch, and she could not speak English. She was beaten because she could not understand the Nealys' orders. Her father learned that she was being treated badly and begged another man to buy her from the Nealys.

An auctioneer (standing on the table) tries to sell a baby, as the baby's mother, a slave, begs to have her baby returned to her. Many black families were separated forever by the evils of slavery.

A husband and wife jump over a broomstick together, an old practice at weddings. Sojourner and Thomas had a marriage ceremony in 1814, but they could not be lawfully married. Slaves were not considered to be U.S. citizens.

A Young Marriage

Sojourner was almost 17 years old and 6 feet (2 m) tall when she worked for a man named John Dumont. He was her fourth owner. She worked in fields planting corn, caught fish, worked in the kitchen, and cared for the Dumonts' children. In 1814, Sojourner agreed to marry a man named Thomas. Thomas was also a slave on the Dumont farm. Within 12 years, Sojourner and Thomas had four daughters and a son.

In 1827, New York passed an **emancipation** law. Slaves born before July 4, 1799, would be free on July 4, 1827. Dumont refused to let her go free, so Sojourner escaped and became a paid servant for the Van Wageners, a **Quaker** family.

13

Saving Peter from Slavery

After she went to work for the Van Wageners, Sojourner learned that John Dumont had sold her six-year-old son, Peter, to Solomon Gedney. Gedney sent Peter to a **plantation** owner in Alabama. Southern states had no emancipation laws. Unless he was rescued, Peter would be a slave forever. Sojourner's friends advised her that slave owners were not allowed to send any slaves to be sold out of New York State. With the help of Quakers, Sojourner filed a **lawsuit** against Gedney, who still claimed that he owned Peter. The judge ruled that Gedney had broken the law and Peter must be returned to Sojourner. She was one of the first black women in the United States to win a lawsuit.

Female slaves and children worked with men in the cotton fields. On July 4, 1827, New York State freed all slaves born before July 4, 1799. Slaves born after 1799 were to be freed at the age of 28, for males, and at the age of 25, for females.

House servants usually could earn more money working in New York City than in the surrounding towns or upstate. In 1828, Sojourner found a paid job as a house servant for a merchant in New York City.

Freedom!

In July 1827, Sojourner Truth was, by law, a free woman. She moved to New York City with her son, Peter. She had to leave behind her other children. Servants were paid better in New York. Sojourner hoped to earn enough money to buy a house where, someday, she would be able live with all of her children. In 1839, Peter was old enough to find work on a whaling ship. Sojourner's older daughters also had moved on and had found work of their own. Sojourner believed it was time for her to move on, too. She had grown tired of living in New York City. She told her employers, "The Lord is going to give me a new home." Sojourner decided to become a traveling preacher.

A New Name

When Sojourner became a traveling preacher in 1843, she chose a name that would not remind her of her days as a slave. She chose the name Sojourner because it meant traveler. She planned to travel around the country to preach God's Word. Truth became her last name because she believed it was a good name for God's **pilgrim**. As she walked through many areas of New York State, farmers stopped their work to listen to her. She was an exciting speaker. Sojourner could not read or write, but people claimed that she knew every word of the Bible. She worked at small jobs to support herself. By the 1850s, she had begun to speak for women's rights and against slavery.

Sojourner Truth met President Abraham Lincoln on October 29, 1864, at the White House in Washington, D.C. He signed her "Book of Life," a book that contained the signatures of many of the people she had met throughout her life.

Frederick Douglass, whom Sojourner Truth met, was a former slave who taught himself to read and write. He became a major leader in the abolitionist movement. He urged Sojourner to continue her fight against slavery.

Speaking Out

Years before Sojourner's travels as a preacher, she had met Frederick Douglass, an abolitionist. He was among a growing number of people who worked for the freedom and equality of everyone who lived in the United States. That meant giving freedom to black people who were still slaves on Southern plantations, and giving women the right to vote. In the late 1840s, Sojourner fought to end slavery in America. Her story, *The **Narrative** of Sojourner Truth: A Northern Slave*, was **published** in 1850. It described the cruelty of slavery. She was able to support herself by selling copies of the narrative. In 1857, she had enough money to buy land and build a house in Battle Creek, Michigan.

On the Road with a Message

Sojourner traveled to small towns across the western United States, where few black people lived. She wanted to bring the message to people there about the evils of slavery. In her travels, she learned that, in some ways, women were not as free as men. They did not have the right to vote in national elections, for example. She became a feminist, speaking at women's rights **conventions**. She believed that a woman was not a citizen without the right to vote. "I must sojourn once to the **ballot box** before I die," she said. She never had a chance to vote, though. On November 26, 1883, Sojourner Truth died in Battle Creek, 37 years before women won the right to vote.

Glossary

abolitionist (a-buh-LIH-shun-ist) A person who worked to end slavery.
auctioned (AWK-shund) A public sale at which goods are sold. During the time of slavery, people were sold at auctions.
ballot box (BAL-ut BOX) The box in which votes are placed.
civil rights (SIH-vul RYTS) The rights of citizens regardless of their race, age, religion, or sex.
conventions (kun-VEN-shunz) Formal meetings for a special purpose.
emancipation (ih-man-sih-PAY-shun) The giving of freedom.
feminist (FEM-uh-nist) A person who works for the economic, political, and social equality of women.
lawsuit (LAW-soot) A case held in a court.
legend (LEH-jend) A story passed down through the years that many people believe, but that might not be true.
masters (MAS-turz) During slavery, slave owners.
narrative (NAR-uh-tiv) A story, or the telling of a story.
pilgrim (PIL-grim) A person who searches for a sacred or holy place.
plantation (plan-TAY-shun) A very large farm. Many plantations had slaves to work these farms.
published (PUH-blishd) When something, such as a book, story, or poem, has been printed so people can read it.
Quaker (KWAY-kur) A person who belongs to a religion that believes in equality for all people, in strong families, and in peace.

Index

A
abolitionist, 6, 21

B
Baumfree, Elizabeth (mother), 9
Baumfree, James (father), 9
Baumfree, Peter (brother), 9

C
changing her name, 9, 18
civil rights, 5

D
Douglass, Frederick, 21
Dumont, John, 13, 14

E
emancipation, 13, 14

F
feminist, 6, 22

G
Gedney, Solomon, 14

N
Narrative of Sojourner Truth: A Northern Slave, The, 21
Nealys, the, 10

Q
Quaker(s), 13, 14

S
slave(s), 5, 9, 13, 14, 18, 21

T
Thomas (husband), 13
traveling preacher, 17, 18, 21

V
Van Wageners, the, 13, 14

W
women's rights, 5, 18, 22

Web Sites

To learn more about Sojourner Truth, check out these Web sites:
http://museumstuff.com/learn/truth.html
www.sojournertruth.org/